THE USBORNE BOOK OF MASKS

Ray Gibson

Edited by Paula Borton • Designed by Ian McNee
Illustrated by Chris Chaisty • Photographs by Ray Moller
Series editor : Cheryl Evans

With thanks to Noorece Ahmed, Eliza Borton, Joanna Borton, Jessica Borton, Rebecca Treays, Maria Wheatley and Marie-Lou Cousin

Contents

First published in 1993. Usborne Publishing Ltd., Usborne House, 83-85, Saffron Hill, London EC1N 8RT, England. Copyright © 1993 Usborne Publishing Ltd. First published in America in March 1994. The name Usborne and the device ☺ are Trade Marks of Usborne Publishing Ltd. All rights reserved. No part of this publication may be reproduced, stored in a retrieval system or transmitted in any form or by any means, mechanical, photocopying, recording or otherwise, without the prior permission of the publisher. Printed in Portugal UE.

Making masks

Before you start, it is a good idea to gather everything you need. The photograph on the right shows you the basic materials and equipment for mask-making, while the special things you need are listed in the introduction to each mask.

You can find PVA glue* and paper reinforcement rings in stationers' or office supply stores. If you don't have tracing paper you can use greaseproof paper, while some food packaging provides a good supply of thin cardboard.

*You can buy hat and shirring elastic** in dressmakers' stores.*

Fastening your mask

There are three different ways of fastening your mask, depending on its shape, and whether it is heavy or light.

Hat elastic

Hat elastic is thin, but very strong and is good for fastening heavy masks. You need a piece about 25cm (10in) long to fasten one mask. See right for how best to attach this elastic.

1. Poke small holes with a pencil. Do this 1cm (½in) from the sides and level with the eyeholes.

2. On the inside of the mask, stick paper reinforcement rings over the holes. This prevents any tears.

3. Thread the elastic through both holes and knot the ends at the edges. Tape down the loose ends.

Shirring elastic

This fine elastic is good for lighter masks. These masks have slits in the sides for you to wind the elastic through. You will need about 25cm (10in) for each mask.

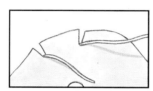

1. Slide the elastic, either side, through the top slit and around to the bottom. Leave a tail.

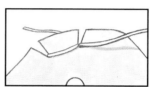

2. Pull each short end up through the top slit and around the front. Pull firmly through the bottom slit.

3. Make sure the elastic fits around your head snugly. Then tape down the loose end on either side.

2

* Household glue (U.S) ** Elastic cord and elastic thread (U.S)

Cardboard strips

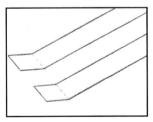

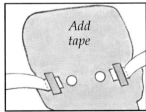

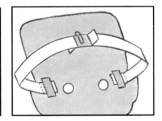

1. Cut two pieces of thin cardboard 30 x 3cm (12 x 1½in). Fold up 2cm (1in) tabs at one end of each.

2. Stick the tabs, using PVA glue, to the back of the mask, 3cm (1½in) away from the eyeholes.

3. Wrap the strips around your head. Add a paper clip to hold the headband together until you tape it.

Cutting eyeholes

Poke the point of a sharp pencil in the middle of the eyehole. Push the blade of your scissors into the hole. Make small snips to the edge before cutting the circle out.

Tracing templates

The shape will appear.

1. Lay a sheet of tracing paper over the template. Slide on a few paper clips.

2. With a pencil, carefully trace all the lines and any special markings.

3. Turn the tracing over and draw thickly with a soft pencil over the outlines.

4. Turn the tracing back over and lay onto paper or cardboard. Pencil over the lines.

Tracing half-templates

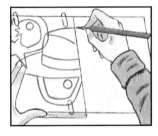

1. Fold a sheet of tracing paper. Open it out and lay the fold on the template's edge.

2. Trace the shape. Take off the tracing and fold it. The lines will show through.

3. Carefully copy the outline showing through. This will complete the shape.

4. Now open out the tracing to see your template. Then follow steps 3-4 above.

Skull

The secret of this creepy mask is to paint it with tea or coffee to make it look really old and decayed. First copy the template on page 31 onto white thin cardboard. You will also need: strong black tea or coffee; shirring elastic and some paints.

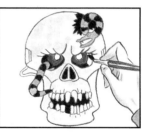

1. Paint over the skull with cold tea or coffee. It's good to leave some blobs and blotches. Now let it dry completely.

2. Go over all the pencil lines in black. Cut out the mask. Snip out the eyeholes and attach the elastic (see pages 2-3).

3. Now paint your mask as shown on the photograph. Try different shades of grey, dirty yellow and brown for the teeth.

Tip

Make these two masks look more lifelike by cutting the lower part of the nose.

Stick the scissor point just below the top of the nose and then carefully cut around.

Stop level with your first cut. The nose will come forward as you put on the mask.

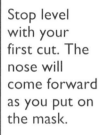

Frankenstein

Everyone will recognize this gruesome monster from films and books. The mask is very dramatic especially if you wear black. Copy the template on page 30 onto white thin cardboard. You also need red, black and brown paints, and more thin cardboard.

1. Carefully cut out the mask. Snip the eyeholes (see page 3). Now go over all the pencil lines with a black felt-tip pen.

2. Cut two strips of cardboard 30 x 3cm (12 x 1½in). Fold back 2cm (1in) for tabs and glue on. Add tape to hold (see page 3).

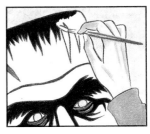

3. Paint the mask as shown on the photograph. When the mask is dry, wrap the strips around your head and tape.

Tip

To give Frankenstein even more character, dab on a little shading. Do this by dipping cotton wool* into some runny dark paint. Wipe the cotton wool* along some spare paper to sop up most of the paint. Then, when almost dry, dab under the eyes and around the mouth. This will give you a subtle shading effect.

5

Hovering bees

For this eye-catching mask, first trace the basic mask template on page 28 onto thin cardboard and then cut it out. To decorate it, you need some bright flowery wrapping paper, 12 thin silver florists' wires*, white paper, shirring elastic, and yellow paper 24 x 3cm (9½ x 1½in).

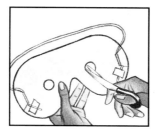

1. Take your mask shape and snip the lines at the sides. Attach elastic and cut out eyeholes as described on page 2-3.

2. Cut out flowers and leaves from the wrapping paper. Glue them onto the mask to cover it completely, as shown below.

3. Cut the wires to lengths of 10 to 15 cm (4 to 6in). Bend the ends of each and tape to the back of the mask, like this.

The bees on this mask will move and hover as you walk around.

Lightly bend the wires, some forwards and some back.

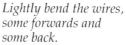

Arranging the flowers

Start at the edge of the mask. Make the first flowers and leaves stick out over the edge.

Move towards the middle of the mask. Glue the flowers on overlapping. Use fewer leaves.

Don't worry if flowers cover the eyeholes. Cut them out again from the back when the glue is dry.

* You can buy these easily and cheaply in your local florists'.

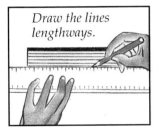

Draw the lines lengthways.

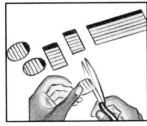

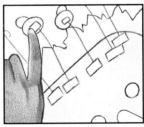

The thick stripe is at the front end.

4. For the bees, draw black lines across the yellow paper with a ruler and a felt-tip pen. Do a really thick line at the top.

5. Cut the paper into twelve 2cm (½in) pieces. Now round off the corners of each piece to make fat bee shapes.

6. Cut out 12 white teardrop shapes from white paper. Glue one onto each bee, slant them slightly away from the front end.

7. Turn over the mask so it is right side down. Slip a bee face down behind the tip of each wire and tape it on.

You can add some glitter to the silver paper.

Give the fish glittery eyes.

Leaping fish

Prepare the same basic mask as before. Use blue cardboard, or paint it. Glue on wavy strips of green and silver paper.

Glue on long, thin points of cardboard for reeds.

Tape wires on (step 3, opposite) and tape fish shapes to their tips.

Octopus

These jolly carnival masks cover your whole head and are very simple to make. For the octopus, cut a piece of vinyl wallpaper 100cm (40in) long and another piece 75cm (30in) long. You will also need green and orange thick paint, a sponge, a stapler and some paper clips.

Plain sides if patterned wallpaper.

1. Dab the wallpaper with a sponge dipped in green paint. Let it dry, then wipe with a damp sponge to get a pale watery look.

Use paper clips to hold.

2. Fold the short edges of the larger piece of paper. Use paper clips to hold the ends together. Draw a large octopus head.

Move paper clips to sides.

3. Carefully cut out the shape, moving the paper clips to the sides. Now staple the edges, leaving the bottom open.

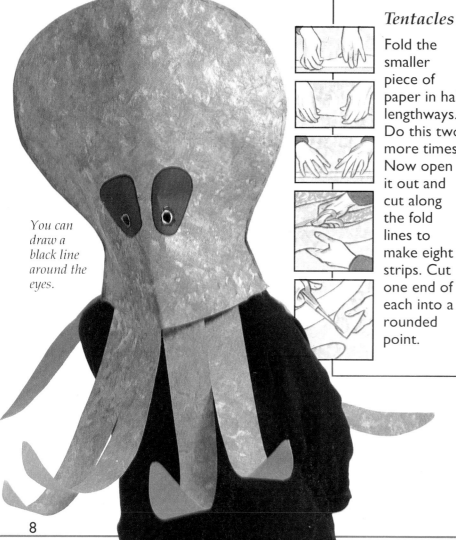

You can draw a black line around the eyes.

Tentacles

Fold the smaller piece of paper in half lengthways. Do this two more times. Now open it out and cut along the fold lines to make eight strips. Cut one end of each into a rounded point.

4. Put the mask on and ask a friend to help you mark places for the eyeholes*. Take off the mask and cut out the eyeholes.

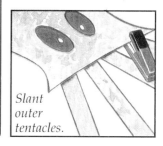

Slant outer tentacles.

5. Paint large orange eyes around the eyeholes. Staple four tentacles onto the back and four onto the front (see left).

*Take care not to hurt your eyes.

Clown

This clown is made in much the same way as the octopus. Cut a piece of wallpaper 100cm (40in) long and fold the short edges. Draw a clown's head and then cut it out (see steps 2-3 on page 8). You will also need some bright crêpe paper and a piece of cardboard.

Any pattern goes on the inside.

1. Cut long crêpe paper strips 6cm (2½in) wide. Pleat and staple them around the edge of one head shape.

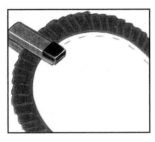

2. Place the other head shape on top of the frilled half and staple the edges together. Keep the plain side up.

3. Cut eyeholes (see step 4 on page 8) and then paint on a mouth around them. Add a nose, eyes and eyebrows.

You can use glitter pen to outline eyes, mouth and nose.

4. Cut a piece of stiff cardboard about 12 x 7cm (5 x 3in) and glue, as shown, to the inside bottom edge of the mask.

5. Tie a huge bow out of crêpe paper. Now glue it to the cardboard that is hanging down at the front of the mask.

9

Fiery dragon

To make this ferocious-looking mask you need: thin red cardboard; orange crêpe paper; yellow, white and black paint; green glitter (if you like) and shirring elastic.

Although it is so dramatic, this mask is quick and easy to make. Trace and cut out the shape in thin cardboard using the template on page 32. Go over the cutting lines on the face in blue. This makes it easier to see where to cut.

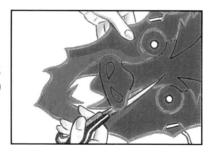

1. Snip out the eyeholes and attach the elastic (see pages 2-3). Cut along all the blue lines. See the tip box for cutting hints. Paint the face.

2. When the paint is dry, go around all the features in black. Dab a little glue around the eyes and scatter on green glitter, if you like.

Cutting the mask

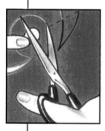

Cut along the blue lines. Poke a hole with the point of your scissors to start off.

Fold along the dotted lines and pinch the cardboard back. This helps the features to pop out.

The nose, brows and eyes come forward to make the mask look really dramatic.

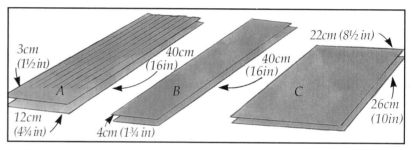

3. Cut two pieces of crêpe paper to each of the sizes shown above. Snip along the pieces called A up to 3cm (1½in) from the end.

4. Snip the pieces called B up to 2cm (1in) from the end; and then snip the pieces called C up to 9cm (3½in) from the end.

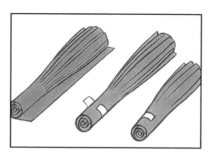

5. Tightly roll up each strip at the short uncut end and stick tape over the join to hold together. Use two shades of crêpe paper, if you like:

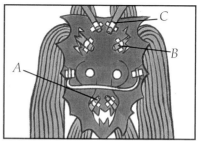

6. Tape pieces A behind the nostrils; pieces B behind the brows; pieces C at the top of the mask. Then tease the tassels around the mask.

You can add foil to eyes and add extra markings to give more expression. Tape on extra tassels if you like.

Detective

Before you start this mask, cut out a basic mask shape from thin cardboard using the template on page 28, and set aside. You will also need: thin cardboard; piece of black plastic; black paint; a thick black felt-tip pen and hat elastic. You can attach this the same way as shirring elastic if you like (see page 2).

1. Copy the template on page 29 onto thin cardboard. Go over the lines in black (keep the tracing to use later).

2. Cut around the shape and snip out the eyeholes. Paint the hatband and frame of the glasses with black paint.

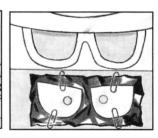

3. Cut out the lenses of the glasses from your tracing and lay them onto a piece of black plastic. Use paper clips to hold.

Put on a big raincoat with padded shoulders.

4. Cut around the pieces. Then snip out the eyeholes; bend the pieces back to make the job easier. Glue the lenses onto the mask.

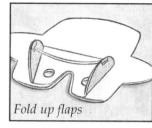

Fold up flaps

5. Glue the front of the basic mask to the back of the main mask. Attach elastic to the flaps.

Paint some stubble on your face to finish off the disguise.

Movie star

This glamorous mask is great fun for when you want to dress up. Make it in the same way as the detective. First cut out a basic mask out of thin cardboard using the template on page 28. You will also need kitchen foil, thin cardboard and a glitter pen to decorate the mask.

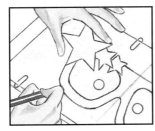

Smooth down.

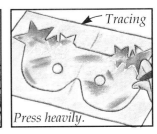

Tracing

Press heavily.

1. Trace and copy the template on page 29 onto a piece of thin cardboard. Keep the tracing as you will need it later.

2. Carefully cut out the shape. Spread glue over the front of the mask then lay it face down onto a piece of foil.

3. Turn over the mask and trim the edges and eyeholes. Lay the tracing over the top and pencil over the stars so they stand out.

Add more glitter to the mask for a really sparkly effect.

4. See steps 3-5 opposite for how to stick on the black plastic lenses, and how to attach the basic mask with elastic.

5. Go around all the edges and points of the stars with glitter pen.

13

Tiger

Use the templates on pages 24-25 to copy the shape of this fierce tiger. You can make other animals from the big cat family, such as a panther, leopard or lion, using the same templates. To make the tiger you will need orange stiff paper; thin white cardboard to make whiskers; black, white, yellow and red paints. Use the photograph as a guide for painting the mask.

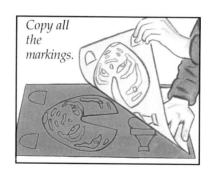

Copy all the markings.

1. Cut out all the shapes copied from the template. Snip out the eyeholes (see pages 2-3 for help on doing all this).

Use paper clips to hold until dry.

2. Take the ears and turn one over to make a left and right ear. Bend the inner corner of each and glue down. Let them dry.

Mix red and white paints for the pink nose.

Painting the eyes

Use a thin paintbrush. Paint the iris yellow and then let it dry.

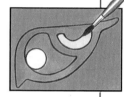

Add the black outline and paint in the pupil.

Paint white around the eyeholes.

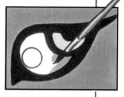

You could add white highlights to the pupil.

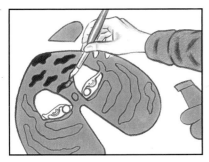

3. Paint the pieces; you can use the photograph as a guide. Outline the features in black. Look at the box on the left for help painting the eyes.

Back of mask

4. Glue the ears behind the face, between the marks at the top. Place the ears so that the folded sides face each other. Let the glue dry.

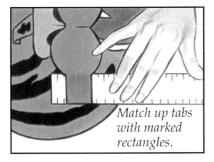

Match up tabs with marked rectangles.

5. Fold down all the tabs on the muzzle and glue them onto the face. Press the tabs down with the end of a ruler so you don't squash the shape.

Cut out and stick on long black or white whiskers.

Panther

Use black paper. Glue on a piece of black plastic to make a shiny nose. Paint the iris bright yellow and add light brown around the eyeholes. Paint the mouth red and the teeth white. Cut six small tapering strips out of black paper and glue them, three each side, pointing up just above the eyes.

Leopard

Use light brown paper and paint on black spots. Paint the eyes yellowish-green.

Lion

Use brown paper. Before adding the headband, glue the mask onto a large piece of brown paper and draw and cut out a shaggy mane. Paint the eyes yellow.

6. Make a headband out of strips of orange paper (see page 3 for how to do this). Make sure it fits your head snugly before you tape it.

Whiskers

Cut long, thin pointed whiskers in different lengths from white cardboard.

Glue the unpointed ends onto the muzzle. Paint on black dots as shown.

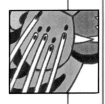

Wolf

To make this wolf mask, copy and cut out the templates on pages 26-27. You need: a large sheet of dark grey stiff paper; light grey stiff paper 16 x 16cm (6½ x 6½in); a piece of thin white cardboard; toilet tissue; a spongy cleaning cloth and some black plastic for the nose.

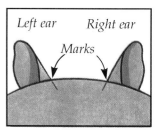

Add paper clips until dry.

Left ear   *Right ear*
Marks

1. Carefully cut out the eyeholes (see page 3 for how to do this), then copy the photograph to paint the eyes. Let it dry.

2. Make the headband (see below). Turn over one ear to make a left and right ear. Bend the inner corners in and glue.

3. When dry, glue the ears behind the mask. Line them up with the marks. Make sure you put them on the correct sides.

Headband

Cut two strips of dark grey paper 30 x 3cm (12 x 1½in). Fold back 2cm (1in) on each as tabs.

Glue the tabs to the back of the mask, with the edges level with the eyes and 3cm (1½in) away.

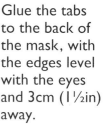

Add tape to hold. To fit, overlap bands around your head. Paper clip together, then tape.

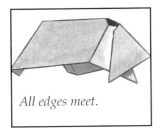

All edges meet.

4. Take the muzzle. Bend the fold lines down. Glue the front pieces together on top of each other for the muzzle shape.

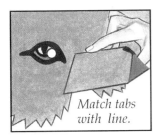

Match tabs with line.

5. Glue the tabs on the muzzle and stick it onto the face. Glue the teeth onto the inside of the muzzle, at the front.

Brown bear

Cut out the templates on pages 26-27 using brown paper. Make the mask in the same way as the wolf. Paint the inner ears.

Stick both corners of the ears down 1cm (½in) before gluing. Stick on beige or cream eyebrows, but don't paint eyes.

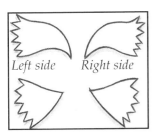

Left side   Right side

6. Take the brow and cheek pieces and lay them out, as shown. Cut four small squares of sponge cleaning cloth.

7. Glue a square of sponge cloth to the back of all the pieces to make them stand out from the face. Stick them on.

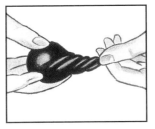

8. Roll a little toilet tissue into a ball and wrap it in the black plastic. Twist the ends tightly and wind with a strip of tape.

9. Push the twisted end into the hole in the snout to make a nose. Then attach it to the inside of the mask with some tape.

Bright bird

This vivid bird mask is very comfortable to wear. Make a basic mask out of thin cardboard using the template on page 28. You also need a piece of thin cardboard 18 x 8cm (7 x 3in); about ½ metre (1½ft) medium weight sew-in interfacing*; red and yellow paint and shirring elastic.

Draw around a tumbler.

1. Cut two pieces of interfacing 45 x 8cm (17¾ x 3in), one piece 20 x 9cm (8 x 3½in) and two circles, 8cm (3in) across.

2. Dip the two pieces of the same size into cold water and squeeze them. Blot the pieces between newspaper .

3. With a fat paintbrush drip yellow and red runny paint onto the damp pieces. The paint will smudge slightly.

The beak

Fold your piece of thin cardboard so the long sides meet. Mark the bottom edge 3cm (1¼in) from the left.

Join the points called A, B and C with a pencil line. Cut along the lines.

Snip 1cm (½in) along the top of the fold and bend the sides to make tabs. Paint it orange and let it dry.

* You can buy interfacing in dressmakers' stores.

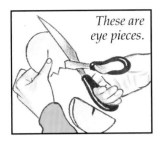

These are eye pieces.

4. Fold the circles in half and snip the middles. Open them out and snip points around the edge of each circle.

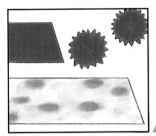

5. Paint the circles and the remaining piece of interfacing bright red. Let all the painted pieces dry in a warm place.

Paint black circles on the eye pieces to outline the eyes.

Owl

The owl mask is made in the same way as the bright bird. Use runny brown paint for the speckled feathers and paint the top feathers brown. Paint the eye pieces white. Make a shorter, fatter beak using the template on page 24.

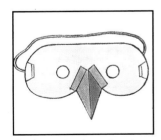

6. Attach the elastic to the basic mask (see page 2). Glue the tabs of the beak 3cm (1¼in) from the top (see box left).

Cut lots of strips together.

7. Cut the spotted pieces and the red piece into 2½cm (1in) strips. Trim them to make rounded points like feathers.

8. Glue four red feathers each side, then five spotted ones either side. Stick three straight up and two down.

9. Glue the rest of the feathers around the eyes and stick on the eye pieces, as shown. Push the scissors into the eye slit to cut out.

19

Goggle-eyed monster

For this mask you need:
two eggs; yellow and white
poster paints; green tissue
paper- one piece 28 x 40cm
(11 x 16in), one 30 x 16cm
(12 x 6in) and two 22 x 27cm
(9 x 11in); two sequins and
kitchen foil. First trace the
mask shape from page 28
onto thin cardboard. Cut it
out, snipping out the
eyeholes (see page
3). Then make
eyeballs as
shown
right.

*Place strips
on line.*

*Add tape
when glue
is
dry*

Back

1. Rule across above the
eyeholes. Glue on strips of
cardboard for the headband
(see page 3 for how to
do this).

*Short edge lines up
with top.*

2. Spread glue over the front
of the mask. Line up a short
edge of the largest piece of
tissue with the top. Pinch
wrinkles as you press down.

*You can
paint on
a red circle
to make the
eyes look
really startling.*

Making the eyeballs

Lightly boil the
eggs. When
cool, break or
cut off the
narrow end of
each egg, and
scoop out the
yolk and white.

Wash and dry
the big halves.
Trim the edges
to make them
level. Paint with
white mixed
with PVA glue.
Let them dry.

scissor.

Add PVA glue
to yellow paint.
Paint a circle on
top of the eyes.
Press a sequin
onto the wet
paint.

Stick tape half on mask and half on sides of egg.

Pleat on short edges.

These are eyelids.

Try not to crush pleats in the eyelids.

3. When dry, trim the eyeholes and the edges of the mask. Tape the eyeballs above the eyeholes, keeping them level with the strips.

4. Fold the pieces of tissue 22 x 27cm (9 x 11in) into concertina pleats. Fold them in half and pinch the fold. Glue the loose ends together.

5. Glue around the eggs and 2cm (1in) up the sides. Place the eyelids over the eggs, try not to crush the pleats. Press gently onto the mask.

Cyclops

Cyclops was a one-eyed Greek monster.

Use the same steps to make a Cyclops mask, like this, or a three-eyed monster.

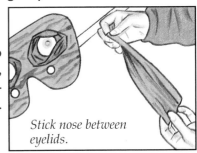

Stick nose between eyelids.

6. Fold the short edges of the last piece of tissue together. Pleat the folded end, squeeze and fold back 2cm (1in). Glue to the mask.

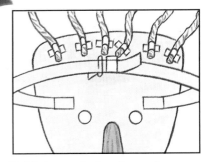

7. Make weird twists of kitchen foil to tape behind the top of the mask. Wrap the strips around your head (see page 3).

Dracula

This mask is shaped onto a clay base which you can use again and again. You will need a shallow bowl about 15cm (6in) across; a tray; clingfilm; about 1kg (2lb) self-hardening clay; kitchen foil; a cotton wool ball*; white tissue paper; black yarn; hat elastic and black and red paints.

1. Turn the bowl over and put it on the back of the tray. Cover it all with clingfilm. Roll balls of clay about the size of small oranges.

2. Flatten the balls and press them over the bowl. Add a larger ball at one end to shape a chin. Smooth the joins with your thumbs.

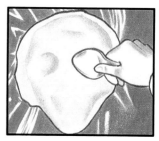

3. About half-way down the face, press in eye sockets with the back of a dessert spoon. Rock the spoon from side to side as you press.

You could paint the eyes like this. Use glitter pen for Dracula's shiny eyeballs.

Add a few drops of red to the fangs.

Eyes
Slightly flatten two marble-sized balls of clay into the sockets.

Eyebrows
Roll sausage shapes. Place them so that they arch.

Lips
Taper the ends of two sausage shapes. The bottom lip should be slightly shorter than the top. Press curves in the top lip. Roll and press on two fangs.

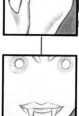

Nose
Make a wedge and pinch it along the top. Smooth two small balls onto each side of the nose for nostrils. Poke your finger in to shape them.

*cotton ball (US)

4. Shape Dracula's features and firmly press them on the face (see box left). Leave in a warm place overnight to dry.

5. Lay foil over the face and press it down, starting with the nose (see Tips). Flatten the creases with cotton wool*.

Sea witch

On the clay base, leave out the fangs and make the mouth smaller. Glue on blue or green tissue paper instead of white. Stick blue glitter on the brows, eyes and mouth. Tape on strips of shiny green paper and gift wrap ribbon for the hair. Glue on shiny cut-out fish.

Tips

If the kitchen foil rips while you are pressing it around the clay base, just dab some glue around the tear and then patch it with a small piece of foil.

As you stick on the tissue paper, add extra squares on the nose, mouth and brows as well as strips along the sides. This makes the mask really strong.

6. Paint PVA glue over the face and around the base. Stick on small squares of tissue paper. Do this four times (see Tips).

7. When dry, ease the mask off the clay base. Trim the mask, leaving a 1cm (½in) edge. Turn in the edges and press.

8. Poke in eyeholes with a sharp pencil and add hat elastic (see page 2). Glue on yarn strands in a V-shape for hair.

9. With a nearly dry brush, shade around the eyes in red and then paint them as shown. Paint the lips red and the brows black.

Templates

For lots of the masks you need to trace the templates (outline shapes) on the next few pages. Look at page 3 for help doing this.

Don't forget to read all the instructions on the templates.

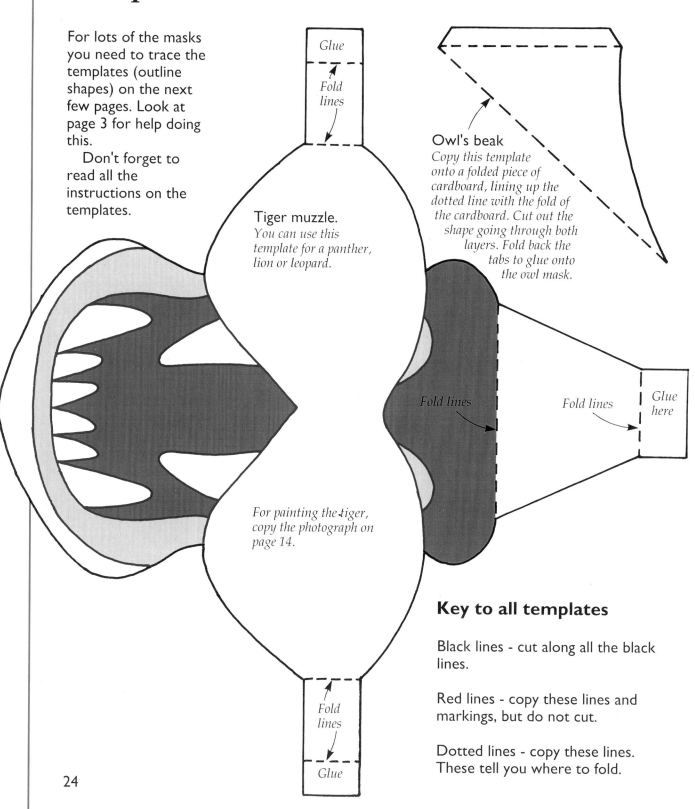

Glue

Fold lines

Tiger muzzle.
You can use this template for a panther, lion or leopard.

Owl's beak
Copy this template onto a folded piece of cardboard, lining up the dotted line with the fold of the cardboard. Cut out the shape going through both layers. Fold back the tabs to glue onto the owl mask.

Fold lines

Fold lines

Glue here

For painting the tiger, copy the photograph on page 14.

Fold lines

Glue

Key to all templates

Black lines - cut along all the black lines.

Red lines - copy these lines and markings, but do not cut.

Dotted lines - copy these lines. These tell you where to fold.

Tiger ears
Copy and cut out two of these.

Fold

Glue

Panther

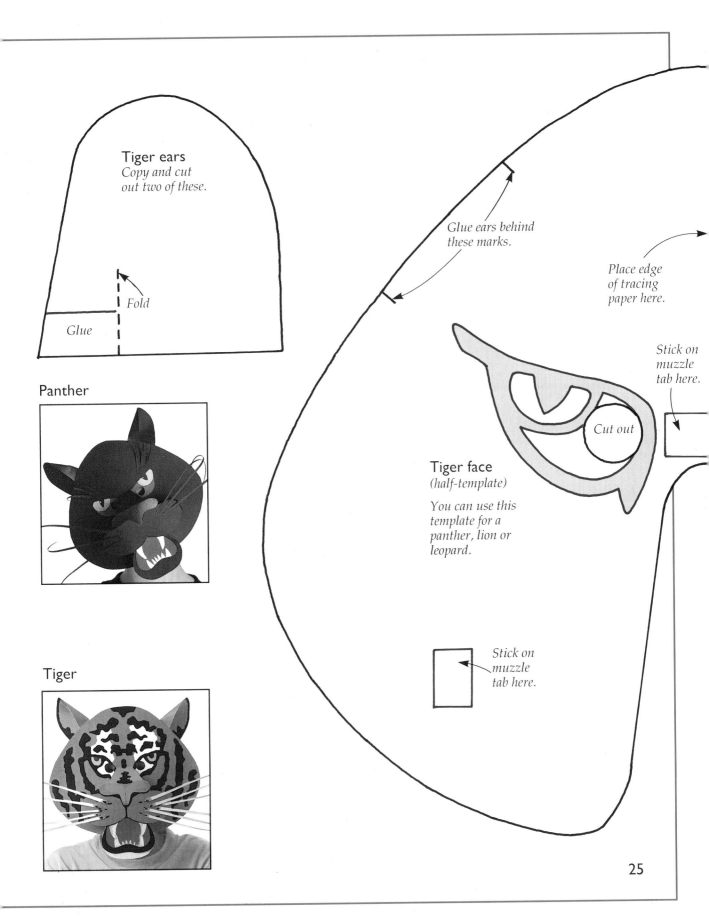

Tiger

Glue ears behind these marks.

Place edge of tracing paper here.

Stick on muzzle tab here.

Cut out

Tiger face
(half-template)

You can use this template for a panther, lion or leopard.

Stick on muzzle tab here.

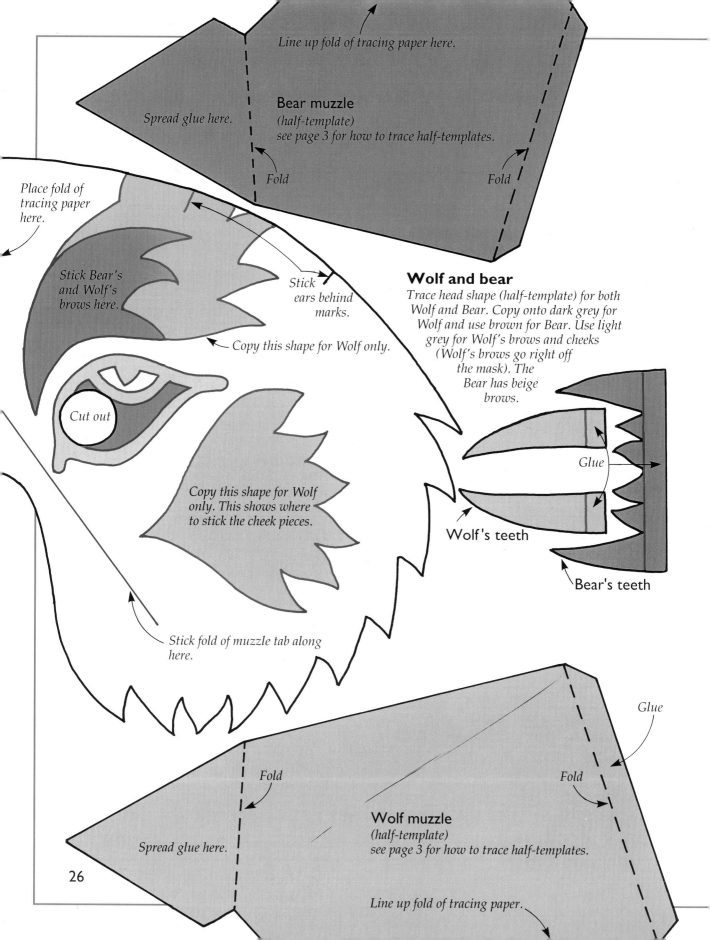

Line up fold of tracing paper here.

Bear muzzle
(half-template)
see page 3 for how to trace half-templates.

Spread glue here.

Fold

Fold

Place fold of
tracing paper
here.

Stick Bear's
and Wolf's
brows here.

Stick
ears behind
marks.

Wolf and bear
*Trace head shape (half-template) for both
Wolf and Bear. Copy onto dark grey for
Wolf and use brown for Bear. Use light
grey for Wolf's brows and cheeks
(Wolf's brows go right off
the mask). The
Bear has beige
brows.*

Copy this shape for Wolf only.

Cut out

Copy this shape for Wolf
only. This shows where
to stick the cheek pieces.

Glue

Wolf's teeth

Bear's teeth

Stick fold of muzzle tab along
here.

Glue

Fold

Fold

Wolf muzzle
(half-template)
see page 3 for how to trace half-templates.

Spread glue here.

Line up fold of tracing paper.

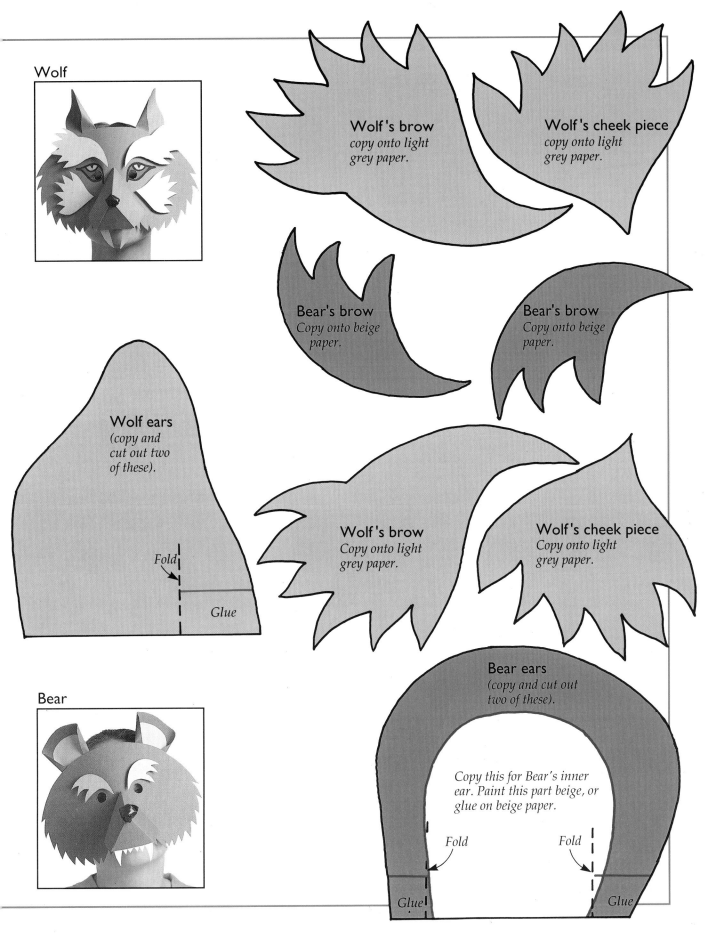

Wolf

Wolf's brow
copy onto light grey paper.

Wolf's cheek piece
copy onto light grey paper.

Bear's brow
Copy onto beige paper.

Bear's brow
Copy onto beige paper.

Wolf ears
(copy and cut out two of these).

Fold

Glue

Wolf's brow
Copy onto light grey paper.

Wolf's cheek piece
Copy onto light grey paper.

Bear ears
(copy and cut out two of these).

Copy this for Bear's inner ear. Paint this part beige, or glue on beige paper.

Fold

Fold

Bear

Glue

Glue

You will need the basic mask
shape on this page to make
lots of the masks in this book.

Goggle-eyed monster

Hovering bee
(You need a basic mask for this)

Leaping fish
(you need a basic mask for this)

Owl
(you need a basic mask for this)

Bright bird
(you need a basic mask for this)

Basic mask
(half-template)

Place fold here.

Cut out

See page 2 for how to attach elastic.

You only need mark the fold lines for the Detective and the Movie star masks.

Fold lines

Place fold here.

Cut out

Goggle-eyed monster
(half-template)

Copy this line for Goggle-eyed monster.

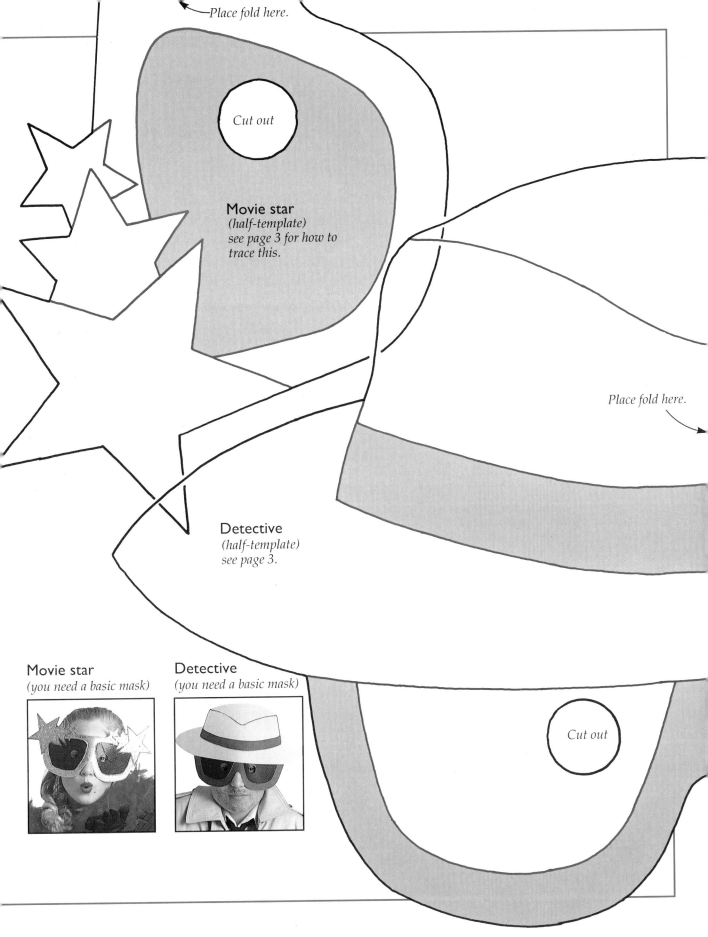

Place fold here.

Cut out

Movie star
(half-template)
see page 3 for how to
trace this.

Place fold here.

Detective
(half-template)
see page 3.

Movie star
(you need a basic mask)

Detective
(you need a basic mask)

Cut out

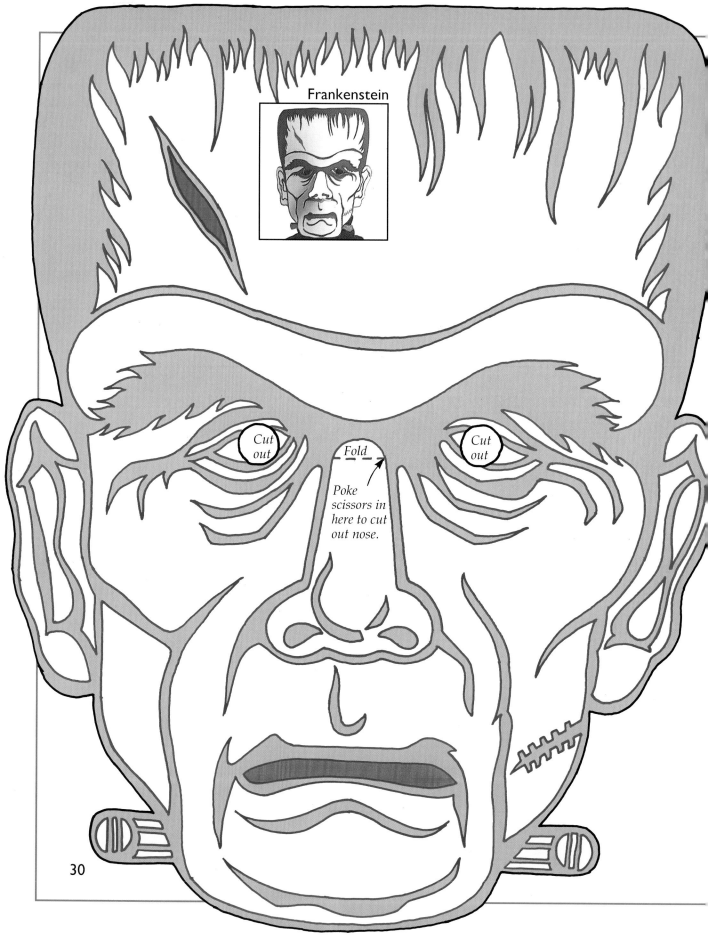

Frankenstein

Cut out

Fold

Cut out

Poke scissors in here to cut out nose.

30

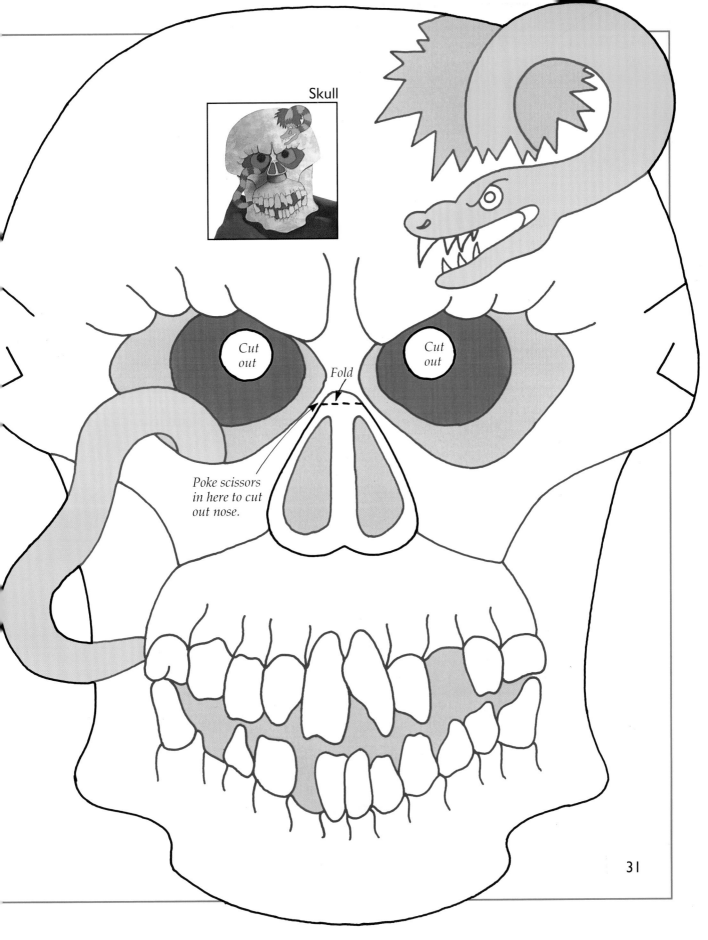

Skull

Cut out

Cut out

Fold

Poke scissors in here to cut out nose.

31

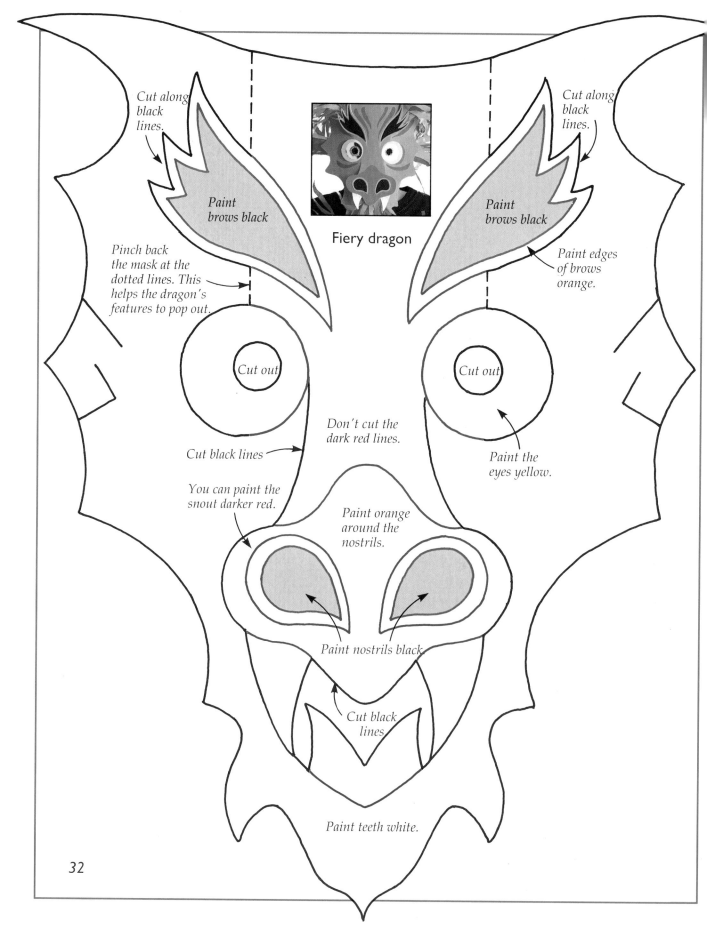

Cut along black lines.

Paint brows black

Fiery dragon

Cut along black lines.

Paint brows black

Paint edges of brows orange.

Pinch back the mask at the dotted lines. This helps the dragon's features to pop out.

Cut out

Cut out

Cut black lines

Don't cut the dark red lines.

Paint the eyes yellow.

You can paint the snout darker red.

Paint orange around the nostrils.

Paint nostrils black.

Cut black lines.

Paint teeth white.